GOOOAAALLL?

By Chris McTrustry

Illustrated by Rob Kiely

GOOOAAALL!

Predict: What do you think this text is going to be about?

I WAS DETERMINED this year would be different.

This year I would be selected for the school soccer team. No more "No thanks, try again next year, Gabriel." This would be my year. After all, great soccer playing was in my blood. I was named after my Uncle Gabriel, who was a star soccer player. He even played for a European soccer team. Sadly, he died in a car accident.

So, I'm determined to carry on the family tradition of soccer stardom!

Unfortunately, my feet don't agree with me. Don't get me wrong, I practice. I like playing. I just don't "get" soccer.

"It'll come to you," my Tata (grandpa) said. He used to be a good player, too, and he's always ready with advice and tips. I'd "hired" him – paying him with odd jobs around his and Abuelita's (grandma's) house – to prepare me for the upcoming tryouts.

A week before the tryouts, I was nosing around in Tata's garden shed. At the back of the shed, I found a pair of old, cracked cleats, abandoned like empty cicada cases.

"Those were your Uncle Gabriel's when he was about your age," Tata said when I showed them to him. "Try them on." He grinned. "Maybe a little of his magic will rub off on you."

...ABANDONED LIKE EMPTY CICADA CASES...

Simile or Metaphor?

Simile – a simile compares one thing to an by using the words "like" or "as," and of creates a mental picture in the reader's m

Metaphor – a metaphor compares one th to another without using the words "lik or "as," and often creates a mental picture in the reader's mind.

So... I put the cleats on. And do you know what? When I had Uncle Gabriel's cleats on my feet, I DID feel real different. Confident. Balanced. Focused.

I tried some of the dribbling tricks Tata had shown me.

"Hey! What do you know?!" Tata whooped. "I think you've got it! Kewell, or even Viduka couldn't have done that move better!"

I didn't say anything, but I knew that a little of Uncle G's "magic" must have seeped into the cracked leather of the cleats.

Gabriel trying on Uncle G's cleats

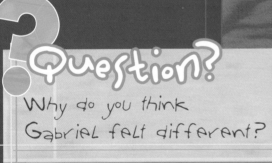

?Question?

Why do you think Gabriel felt different?

Gabriel trying
some tricks

ACTION
AND
RESPONSE
CHART

Action	Response
Gabriel put his cleats on	Confident, balanced, and focused

**Find another action
and response.**

For the rest of the week, I practiced like nobody's business. Tata watched from the sidelines like a hawk surveying its prey.

"Stick to the basic stuff," Tata advised me.

I watched soccer videos (wearing Uncle G's magical cleats), and concentrated hard on positional play.

"A lot of young guys just chase the ball," Tata said. "If you stay in position or anticipate where the ball's going to go, you can get a lot of kicks. Think before you run. Think before you kick."

I nodded my head. "Good idea, Tata."

?Question?

I practiced like nobody's business.

What does this mean?

Gabriel practicing his move

"THINK BEFORE YOU KICK."

SURVEYING

Which is the synonym?

A observing carefully

B glancing

C looking

A, B, or C ?

Gabriel and Tata

Video time!

?Question?

Why do you think Gabriel watched the videos with his cleats on?

Monday morning was the day. Soccer tryouts.

"What are you doing here, Gabriel?" Marco Cavallaro smirked sarcastically. "Trying out for Team Orange Peeler?"

Before I could think of a comeback, Mr. Timpano, the team coach, called us together. "Okay, boys," he said. "Some of you won't make the team, but don't be disappointed. Do your best and play fair."

Okay. I'll cut straight to the BIG news. I got picked. Yes! I was on the school soccer team. And it was all thanks to Uncle G's "magical" cleats.

Mr. Timpano couldn't believe my improvement. He called me "a hardworking midfielder, with loads of flair and potential."

Trying out for Team orange Peeler
What does this mean?

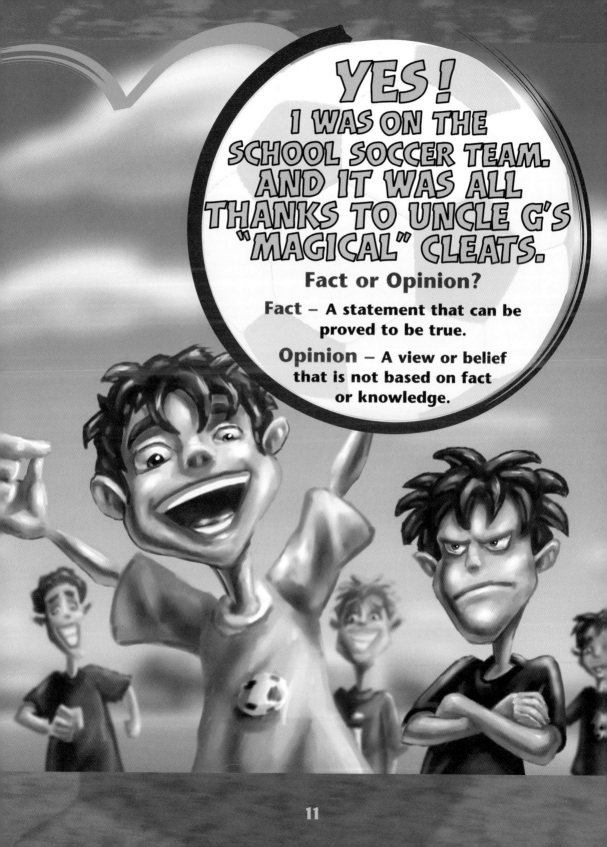

During the games, I stuck to my position like a limpet sticks to a rock. I let Uncle G's cleats guide me. I set up a lot of goals for our team. But what I really wanted was to score my own goal. How cool would that be?!

Unbelievably, we fought our way into the finals of the district competition! The whole school was coming to watch us play Cairncross, a school with an excellent soccer team.

CHARACTER PROFILE

What words best describe Gabriel?

ambitious	pessimistic
determined	nervous
calm	selfish
courteous	positive
excitable	optimistic

WE FOUGHT OUR WAY

Imagery –
The use of words by
the writer to create a
picture in the reader's
mind

... LIKE A LIMPET
STICKS TO
A ROCK ...

Use the imagery of the text
to create your own
mind picture.

INTO THE FINALS!

The day of the finals finally arrived.

I got up early. I was too excited to sleep. I played on the computer. Then I read a book. But all the while I was willing time to move on QUICKLY. The sooner I was at the field, the better.

"Okay, Gabriel," Mom said at last. "Get your cleats. It's time to go."

But my cleats weren't in their usual spot. I couldn't help it – I screamed. LOUD.

Mom and Dad rushed over.

I COULDN'T HELP

?Question?

What can be inferred about Gabriel's character from the words:

"MY CLEATS WEREN'T IN THEIR USUAL SPOT"

It – I Screamed.

"What's the matter?" Mom asked.

"Where are they?" I asked frantically. "I can't find them – my cleats!"

Mom smiled. "That's because Dad and I have a surprise for you."

I frowned. "I don't know if the finals is the day for surprises, Mom… please, can I just have my cleats?"

Dad appeared in the doorway, holding a brightly wrapped box. "Surprise, son!"

"This is our way of saying 'good job'," Mom said.

FRANTICALLY

Which is the synonym?

A excitedly

B desperately

C calmly

A, B, or C ?

Inside the wrapping paper was a shoe box. A cold feeling swept over me like a blast of Arctic wind. Oh no … inside the shoe box was a brand new pair of SOCCER CLEATS.

"Thanks, ummm… but, where are *my* cleats?" I demanded.

"You can't wear those ratty old things in the finals," Mom said. "Everyone will laugh!"

Mom didn't know how right she was. Everyone *would* laugh – at me! I'd play hopelessly without Uncle G's magic cleats.

"YOU CAN'T WEAR THOSE RATTY OLD THINGS IN THE FINALS, … EVERYONE WILL LAUGH!"

What inference can be drawn about Mom from this text?

Well, I wasn't letting anyone down. On the field, I avoided the ball as if it were contaminated. If I didn't kick it, I couldn't do any harm, right?

It must have been obvious, because at half-time, Mr. Timpano said, "Gabriel, if you're trying to lull the Cairncross team into a false sense of security, you've done it. Now start playing – properly." I nodded. "Yes, Coach."

But I continued to avoid the ball. I drifted out onto the left wing and hid. Occasionally the ball would be booted my way. Each time I simply trapped it and punched passes through the center of the Cairncross defense. One of my passes found our center forward, Brad Nguyen. He beat the center and shot. The Cairncross goalkeeper dived full-length and tipped the ball out of play. That was the closest anyone on either team came to scoring.

? Question?
...false sense of security...
What is meant by this?

Late in the game, Wayne Butler ran down the right wing. He beat two defenders and shaped to cross the ball. All of our forwards and midfielders raced into the penalty area, anticipating Wayne's cross. I was going to join them, when suddenly I realized that if the ball was crossed high, Cairncross's center would easily clear it. With most of our team in the Cairncross penalty area, we'd be an easy target for a fast breakaway. I hesitated on the edge.

"What are you doing, Gabriel?" Mr. Timpano yelled. "There's less than a minute left! Get into the penalty area!"

SETTING

Which words would you use to describe the atmosphere at the game?

tense	quiet
dull	noisy
calm	serene
lively	**What else?**

"... LESS THAN

But something – a message from Uncle G's cleats? – told me to stay where I was. And the words of my Tata reverberated in my head – "Think before you run. Think before you kick."

Wayne whipped in a high cross. Marco Cavallaro jumped up to head it, but he was easily beaten by the Cairncross center.

The ball bounced out to me. I measured my stride and smashed the ball back into the penalty area. The ball left my foot like it was jet-propelled and flew into the top right-hand corner of Cairncross's goal.

I, me, Gabriel Gomez, had scored — all by myself — with *my* cleats. Before I knew it, the referee blew for time. We had won!

WE HAD WON!

Clarify!

REVERBERATED

A repeated

B appeared

C bounced

A, B, or C ?

Question?

The ball left my foot like it was jet-propelled...

What does this mean?

Mom and Dad, Tata, and Abuelita hurried up to congratulate me.

"Well done, my boy," Tata grinned. He nodded at my new cleats. "I see you've upgraded your footwear."

"I wanted to wear Uncle G's cleats," I shrugged, "but Mom and Dad got me these for playing so well."

"Good thing, too," Tata said. "You know those 'magic' cleats you found?" I nodded. "They weren't your Uncle Gabriel's after all." He pointed at Dad. "They were your dad's." He laughed. "And he was downright hopeless!"

Select the main points you would include in a summary of Goal.

"MAGIC" CLEATS

THINK ABOUT THE TEXT

Making connections – What connections can you make to the emotions, situations, or characters in *Goal!*?

Text-to-self

AMBITION

DETERMINATION

SUPERSTITION

APPREHENSION

SELF-CONFIDENCE

ANTICIPATION

PRE-GAME TENSION

INTERFERENCE/
SUPPORT FROM FAMILY

DEALING WITH CRITICISM

Text-to-Text

Talk about other stories you may have read that have similar features. Compare the stories.

Text-to-World

Talk about situations in the world that might connect to elements in the story.

PLANNING A SHORT STORY

1 Decide on a storyline

A boy finds an old pair of soccer cleats that he believes belonged to his uncle, a great soccer player.

He thinks that the cleats have "magic" that will make him a great soccer player, too.

He discovers that the cleats actually belonged to someone who didn't play soccer very well.

2 Think about the characters

Think about the way they will think, act, and feel.
Make some short notes or quick sketches.

GABRIEL

enthusiastic
determined
persistent

GRANDPA

supportive
interested
helpful

MOM

concerned
proud
caring

3 Decide on the setting

Make some short notes.

4 Decide on the events in order

Introduction

Events

Climax

SHORT STORIES USUALLY HAVE

A A short introduction that grabs the reader's interest

B Fewer characters than longer stories

C A single fast-moving plot

D A climax that occurs late in the story